Friday
the Scaredy Cat

by Kara McMahon
illustrated by Maddy McClellan

Ready-to-Read

Simon Spotlight
New York London Toronto Sydney

SIMON SPOTLIGHT
An imprint of Simon & Schuster Children's Publishing Division
1230 Avenue of the Americas, New York, New York 10020
Text and illustration copyright © 2011 Simon & Schuster, Inc.
All rights reserved, including the right of reproduction in whole or in part in any form.
SIMON SPOTLIGHT, READY-TO-READ, and colophon are registered trademarks
of Simon & Schuster, Inc.
For information about special discounts for bulk purchases, please contact Simon & Schuster
Special Sales at 1-866-506-1949 or business@simonandschuster.com.
Manufactured in China   0911 SCP

2 4 6 8 10 9 7 5 3
Full Cataloging-in-Publication Data for this book is available from the Library of Congress.
ISBN 978-1-4424-3612-1 (hc)
ISBN 978-1-4424-2293-3 (pbk)
ISBN 978-1-4424-3516-2 (eBook)

This is Friday.

Friday is almost all black.

He has a lot of black fur
and a bit of white fur.

Friday has four big fangs.
Friday is very proud
of his big fangs.

He likes to show them
to everyone he meets.

He calls himself
Friday Fang Dangle.

Some animals are scared
of Friday Fang Dangle!
Friday thinks that is silly.
Friday is not scary!

But Friday is scared
of many things!

Friday is scared
of the doorbell. DING
DONG!

He jumps, runs, and hides.

Friday is scared
of the telephone.

RING!
RING!

He jumps, runs, and hides.

Friday jumps, runs,
and hides.

Friday is scared
of car horns.

HONK!

He jumps, runs, and hides.

Friday is scared of bees.

He jumps, runs, and hides.

Friday may be scared
of many things. . . .

But Friday is not scared
of everything!

Friday knows that some people
are scared of mice.
He thinks that is silly.
Mice are not scary!

Friday is not scared
of dogs.

Friday is not scared
of other cats.

Friday is not scared
of chickens.

Friday is not scared
of bicycles.

But Friday is scared
of chickens
riding bicycles!

Friday is not scared
of the dark.

Not even a tiny bit scared.

He is not scared of ghosts.

BOO!

Friday does not jump,
run, or hide.

Friday smiles at the ghost.

But the ghost is scared
of Friday Fang Dangle!

It jumps, runs, and hides.
Silly scaredy ghost!